Olly Oak

Grosvenor House
Publishing Limited

Imagined by Jon Gilbert
Brought to life by Olivia Wilson

GW01044230

The right of Jon Gilbert to be identified as the author of this
work has been asserted in accordance with Section 78
of the Copyright, Designs and Patents Act 1988

The book cover is copyright to Jon Gilbert
All photos taken by Jon Gilbert, except Winter Oak in Snow – TobyPhotos

This book is published by
Grosvenor House Publishing Ltd
Link House
140 The Broadway, Tolworth, Surrey, KT6 7HT.
www.grosvenorhousepublishing.co.uk

A CIP record for this book
is available from the British Library

ISBN 978-1-78623-552-7

To Maki & Daniel for their support
and encouragement to get Tree Fellas started
and then their patience and advice as this
first story took shape.

It's a cold morning in the forest at the end of winter and the English Oak Tree family wakes up shivering in the snow.

As the sun rises in the clear blue sky, baby saplings, their mums, dads, grandmas and grandpas - some more than 500 years old - wriggle their trunks to shake the snow off their bare branches.

Many have huge, crinkly, silvery-brown trunks and a few are over 30 metres tall, reaching high above the morning mist.

After looking around to make sure you are not watching them, they all start exercises to warm up;

doing sit-ups, stretching, running and jumping on the tips of their roots.

As spring arrives, buds and leaves start growing on their twigs.

The weather gets warmer, and the family dresses in light green coats of new leaves.

Strings of little yellow catkin flowers hang down from the branches of each tree.

Gradually, the leaves turn darker green and the catkin flowers change into little acorns. In summer, Olly Oak grows into a large green acorn near the top of his mother's tree, with his brother and sister snuggled around him.

Every day, when they think you cannot see them, the acorns change into Tree Fellas, and Olly Oak puts on his smart coat of bark, with a cap on his head, ready for an adventure.

As he grows bigger and stronger, he looks down at you and your family walking through the forest. He sees children on bicycles and watches boys and girls playing football.

That looks like fun, thinks Olly Oak, *I'd love to do that*, and he dreams about scoring goals, winning football games and lifting a shiny gold cup with his team.

Then he notices three balls hanging from some leaves below him and asks, "Mum, what are they?"

She tells him, "Those are oak apples which grow on some oak trees every year and drop off in autumn, so you should be able to find a few on the ground when you get down there."

Olly can't wait to discover the new world below.

8

Near the end of summer, Olly is so excited that he decides to leave home as early as possible but does not want to hurt himself when he drops to the ground.

So, when the next puff of wind blows through the branches, Olly Oak grabs a leaf, waves goodbye to his family, lets go of his stalk, and drifts down under his parachute to land softly in the mud.

9

All around him, his brother, sister and Tree Fellas from other English Oak Trees are exploring the forest floor.

Some of them are already turning brown as the weather gets cooler.

He finds an oak apple lying next to his mother's trunk, and thinks, *I can use this as a football.* He kicks it, runs after it, kicks it again and chases it around the grass until he is out of breath and stops for a rest.

Nearby, other Tree Fellas are playing football and suddenly someone kicks their oak apple towards Olly.

He stops it under his foot and passes it back to one of them.

"Great pass", shouts the player, "Come and join the Forest Rovers team!"

Every day they practise passing, dribbling, heading and scoring goals. Forest Rovers play games against teams in the EOL 'English Oak League' from parks, woods and forests all over the country.

Olly Oak becomes a star of the EOL as he scores goal after goal, and Forest Rovers win every single game.

At the end of autumn, English Oak Trees are covered with yellow, gold and brown leaves.

Tree Fellas from all over the country come to watch the FA 'Flying Acorns' Cup Final at Rumbly Stadium.

Forest Rovers wear summer green shirts and Park United are in sunny orange.

Here come the teams!

Kick-off! The game starts, with both teams chasing the ball from end to end of the field, until……

Who scores the first goal?

That's right! Olly Oak jumps high above the Park United players to head the ball into the goal and Forest Rovers lead 1-0.

His family and friends scream with joy, jump up and down and wave their branches wildly.

For the next 30 minutes, Park United try hard
to score a goal and Olly Oak runs up and
down the field to tackle their players and help
Forest Rovers stop them.

There are no more goals,
so the half time score is
Forest Rovers 1
Park United 0

What will happen in the second half?

Oh no! Park United get a goal to make the score 1-1.

Now the Forest Rovers supporters are nervous and worried.
They stamp their roots like thunder to push their team
harder, hoping for another goal.

Only one more minute of the game and the score is still 1-1.

Who will win the FA 'Flying Acorns' Cup?

Here comes Olly Oak running towards goal with the
football and the excited crowd cheers loudly.

Olly Oak dribbles past one player, around another, and kicks the ball past the goalkeeper into the top corner of the goal.

GOOOOOOOOOOOOOOOAL! GO GO GO GOAL!

Forest Rovers lead 2-1 and a few seconds later the referee blows the final whistle to end the game.

Forest Rovers win the FA Cup!

The players hug each other, then run and dance around the field happily. The crowd goes crazy, jumping up and down, wrapping their branches around each other to celebrate.

Olly Oak, hero of Forest Rovers, sits on the shoulders of his team-mates and lifts the gold FA Cup above his head.

Olly's dream has come true.

As winter arrives, Olly Oak turns brown and falls asleep in the dry leaves under his mother's tree, dreaming about that exciting day.

During the next few years, he grows from an acorn into a strong young sapling before becoming an enormous English Oak Tree with a family of his own.

So, next time you are out for a walk, try and find Olly Oak.

Remember that when they hear you coming, Tree Fellas will hide. But if you see green or brown acorns, oak apples or leaves on the ground under a tree, Olly Oak is above you.

Look up, say, "Hello" to Olly Oak and congratulate him on winning the FA Cup.

He will be so happy to see and hear you. Don't forget to pat his trunk and tickle his bark before you wave goodbye. Maybe he will also wave his branches as you leave.

The End

Activities for you to discover more about Olly Oak

Now that you have read the story, here are some activities
to help you find him.

Look at the photos
Keep a Log Book or diary
Learn new facts
Take a quiz
Draw pictures

Take this book with you when you go out for a walk.

At the end of this book, make sure you find out how important
trees are for everybody around the world and how you can help
to save Tree Fellas by planting as many trees as possible.

Look at these pictures to help you find me

Young catkins

Buds

Older catkins

Spring

Acorns

Leaves

Summer

Autumn

Oak apple

Oak apple

Winter

Autumn leaves

Fallen leaves

Can you find me?

Tree trunk

Bark

24

Log Book

1. Where did you meet Olly Oak?
    (in a forest, park, field, garden, street or somewhere else?)

2. How did you know it was Olly?
    (his shape, leaves, catkins, acorns or bark of his trunk?)

3. How many other English Oak Trees could you see?

4. What colour leaves was he wearing, or were they gone?

5. Did you see any catkins, acorns or oak apples?

6. When did you meet him?

Day of the week   Date   Season

_____   _____   _____
Monday, Tuesday...?   Day/Month/Year   Spring, Summer, Autumn, Winter

Did you know...?

- Olly Oak comes from an **English Oak Tree**. It is also called **Common Oak** or **Pedunculate Oak**.

- Its scientific name is **Quercus Robur** which means 'strength' in Latin.

- The wood is one of the hardest, strongest and most long-lasting in the world, and is used for buildings, ships, furniture and more.

- English Oak trees are found all over Britain, Ireland and most of Europe.

- They are **deciduous** trees which lose their leaves in winter. Trees that keep their leaves all year are **evergreen**.

- These large trees can grow up to 20-40 metres high with huge trunks more than 3 metres all the way round.

- English Oaks can live for 800 years or more.

- Trees do not produce acorns until they are at least 40 years old.

- There are hundreds of other types of Oak Trees around the world, so look out for Olly's cousins who might look slightly different.

Olly Oak Quiz

Read the story again to find answers

1. What are baby trees called?

2. How old are some of the Oak trees at the beginning of this story?

3. How tall can English Oak Trees Grow?

4. How many trees are doing exercises?

5. Where do acorns grow from?

6. What colour are catkins?

7. What colour are young acorns?

8. How many Tree Fellas can you see on the branch?

9. How does Olly Oak get down to the ground?

10. What does he find next to his mother's trunk?

11. In autumn, what colours do the leaves change to?

12. Which team does Olly play for?

13. What summer colour are their shirts in the FA Cup Final?

14. What is the name of the other team in the FA Cup Final?

15. How many Tree Fellas are watching the game at Rumbly Stadium?

16. What is the score at half time?

17. Who scores the winning goal?

18. Why do you think Olly is so happy at the end of the game?

19. What colour do acorns change to in autumn?

20. Are English Oak Trees deciduous or evergreen?

Activity – Drawing, Painting & Photo

- Draw Olly Oak when he was a young acorn wearing his cap and coat of bark.

- What will Olly look like when he grows into a huge Oak Tree?

- Find some oak leaves to paint their shapes and colours.

- Add some acorns, catkins and oak apples to your picture.

- Ask someone to take a photo of you with Olly Oak, and stick it in this book.

Have fun!

Olly Oak says...

Tree Fellas need your help!

Why are trees so important to you, your family and friends?

Your health

- Trees are the biggest plants and longest living species on earth
- They provide oxygen for you, animals and plants to keep healthy
- They help to reduce pollution, shade you from the sun and reduce noise
- Woodlands produce food and shelter for animals, birds, insects and more

The environment

- Trees absorb carbon dioxide to help slow down global warming and climate change
- They soak up rain and storm water to help prevent flooding
- Their roots keep the soil firm to help stop erosion and landslides

Your life

- Trees provide timber for building houses, furniture, ships and more
- Woods are great for walking, cycling, birdwatching, exploring and climbing trees

What happens to our planet if we lose trees?

Every year, millions of trees are chopped down around the world as forests are destroyed to sell timber, clear land for farm animals and grow food crops

This deforestation causes dangerous flooding and mudslides to local people who have no more forests for hunting food

Wild, rare animals, plants and insects die when forests disappear

Deforestation and forest fires damage our health, environment and lives!

How can you help?

Choose your tree from a garden centre

Please plant trees to...

Fight climate change & global warming

Prevent flooding & landslides

Reduce air pollution

Improve health

Fight pests & diseases

Thank you

Olly Oak

32

Lightning Source UK Ltd.
Milton Keynes UK
UKHW021008261121
394627UK00005B/59